DIGGING
IN THE
DARK

Other books by Hilda Offen

The Galloping Ghost
Knee-High to a Knight
Nice Work, Little Wolf!
The Trouble with Owls
Watch Out for Witches!
The Wizard's Warning
Rita the Rescuer and Other Stories
Rita and the Romans
Rita at Rushybrook Farm
SOS for Rita
Rita in Rocky Park

DiGGiNG IN THE DARK

*Written and illustrated
by Hilda Offen*

Catnip

For Pat Clarke

CATNIP BOOKS
Published by Catnip Publishing Ltd
14 Greville Street
London EC1N 8SB

This edition first published 2012
1 3 5 7 9 10 8 6 4 2

Text and illustrations © 2012 Hilda Offen

A CIP catalogue record for this book is available from the British Library

ISBN 978-1-84647-139-1

Printed in Poland

www.catnippublishing.co.uk

Chapter 1

'Mum! Mum! Come quick!' It was my sister Izzie, sticking her nose in as usual where it wasn't wanted. 'Josh is trying to set the house on fire.'

Mum came rushing out of the sitting room and grabbed the sheet of paper from me. Then she plunged it into a bowl of water in the sink.

'Mum!' I cried. 'What are you doing? That's my homework!'

'Homework?' snorted Mum. '*Homework*? Setting light to the kitchen? Come off it, Josh! Haven't I told you never to play with matches?'

'Miss Wilson said we had to burn the edges of our letters,' I said. 'To make them look old. Now you've ruined it.'

'I'm sure she didn't tell you to do it in the kitchen,'
said Mum. 'With no adult present.' She held up the
dripping sheet. 'What is this, anyway?'

'I'm meant to be an evacuee in the Second World
War,' I said. 'I'm staying on a farm and I'm writing
home to my family.'

'Huh!' said Izzie, tossing her head. 'If they've got
any sense, they won't reply. And they'll move to
another town as fast as they can.'

'Shut up, Izzie!' I said.

Mum draped my letter over the radiator.

'It'll soon dry,' she said. 'Then you can carry on
with what you're doing. If you're trying to make it
look old, this will probably help. Come on, Izzie –
let's leave him in peace.'

My letter dried in no time. And Mum was right –
the soaking *had* improved it. It was all wrinkled and
stained now. The burnt edges had run into streaks
and a lot of the words were blurred. It looked like
a really ancient letter from an evacuee. I read it
through.

'*Dear Mum,*' it said. '*Here I am on the farm.
I have to milk the cows and plant potatoes. Hope
you're OK. I miss you. But it's really nice to have
a break from my sister.*' I'd underlined the last
sentence in red.

I took my pencil and drew two cows and some
potatoes. Then I drew a matchstick girl with a really
ugly face and wrote 'Izzie' underneath.

I was just admiring my work when there was a
screech of brakes outside and a car door slammed.
Then someone started ringing our bell. Mum

hurried down the hall, with me and Izzie behind her. A dim-looking boy stood on the doorstep, holding a rucksack. It was our cousin Malcolm.

'Hello, Auntie Pat,' he said.

Behind him I spotted Aunt Julia getting back into the car with a strange man, all covered in whiskers.

'Julia!' cried Mum. 'Whatever's up?'

Aunt Julia opened her mouth to reply but the hairy man spoke first.

'We've got to go, Pat,' he said. 'We'll explain later.'

I recognised that voice! It was our uncle Jimmy. He'd grown a beard since I'd seen him last.

'It'll only be for a month or two, Pat,' called Aunt Julia. 'You don't mind looking after Malcolm for a while, do you? He won't be any trouble. We've cleared things with Josh and Izzie's school.'

Then she jumped out of the car again, rushed over and gave Malcolm a big smacking kiss.

'Love you, darling!' she said. 'Love you, love you, love you!'

'Mu-um!' said Malcolm, wriggling around.

Aunt Julia was already darting back to the car. Mum stood there, her mouth opening and shutting like a goldfish. We watched as the car revved up and our aunt and uncle disappeared down the street.

Malcolm stepped into the hall and put down his rucksack. He stood there, his big round glasses flashing in the light.

'Whatever's all this about, Malcolm?' asked Mum.

Malcolm blinked and looked away.

'Please don't ask me, Auntie Pat,' he said. 'My lips are sealed.'

Chapter 2

We all stood there, staring at Malcolm. Izzie was the first to speak. 'What do you mean, "your lips are sealed"?' she said. 'What's happening?'

'I'm not telling you,' said Malcolm, glaring at her.

Izzie looked as though she might be about to move in for the kill, but Mum stopped her.

'Come on, Malcolm,' she said, putting an arm round his shoulders. 'You're very welcome. I daresay you're hungry. Come and have something to eat.'

We all sat and watched our cousin as he ate a cheese sandwich. Then Mum made him a big mug of hot chocolate. She tried ringing Aunt Julia on her mobile, but it was switched off.

'Oh well, you're here now, Malcolm,' she said.

'You'd better sleep in Josh's room. I'll blow up the inflatable bed. Come on, Izzie, you can help me with the sheets.'

'Why me?' asked Izzie, looking cross; but Mum gave her a frown and steered her out of the room.

Malcolm and I stared at each other. I felt a bit lost for words. We didn't see each other very often and I didn't know him that well.

'What have you been up to then, Malc?' I said at last.

'Nothing,' said Malcolm. 'And please don't call me "Malc". I don't like it.'

There was a long silence. Then I tried again.

'Where have your mum and dad gone?' I asked.

Malcolm glared at me.

'I've told you already,' he said. 'I can't say.'

I decided to have one last go at being friendly. I handed him my evacuee's letter, which was lying on the table next to me.

'What's this?' said Malcolm. 'And why's it all dirty and wrinkled?'

'It's my homework,' I said. 'We have to pretend we're evacuees and write home.'

Malcolm sniffed.

'Well that's silly,' he said. 'If you were an evacuee you wouldn't write home on a dirty old bit of paper, would you?'

I thought quickly.

'It was war time,' I said. 'There wasn't much paper around. It was probably an old scrap I found. And I was digging up potatoes at the time – that's why it's dirty.'

'Huh!' said Malcolm.

Then we stopped talking. We sat there for ages, just staring at each other. I decided I didn't like my cousin very much. I was really pleased when Mum and Izzie came back.

'Time for bed, I think,' said Mum. 'Josh – I've given Malcolm your bed as he's the visitor. You can have the inflatable. You don't mind, do you?'

I grunted. A little while ago, I wouldn't have minded at all, but now I *did* mind. Yes, I thought, I minded quite a lot.

Chapter 3

I sat on the inflatable bed and watched as Malcolm unpacked his rucksack. He took out his clothes and laid them neatly on the bed along with his washing things. Then he reached into an outside pocket and took out lots of little bundles, all wrapped in white tissue paper. He started unwrapping them and arranging their contents on the bedside table.

I'd already decided I wasn't going to have much to do with Malcolm, but in the end I couldn't help myself. I peered at Malcolm's display. As far as I could see, there were some old rocks, a chunk of coal, bits of china, some broken glass and some small, crinkled metal things. I couldn't work it out.

'What *are* they?' I asked, peering closer.

Malcolm's eyes gleamed behind his glasses. He looked pleased with himself.

'It's my collection,' he said. 'I'm going to leave it to a museum one day.'

I collected things too – stamps, cards, autographs and even old birds' nests, but nothing like this.

'Collection of *what*?' I asked.

'My finds,' said Malcolm. 'I'm going to be an archaeologist when I grow up. I do digs. I found most of these in our garden.'

He held up a chunk of coal.

'This is a fossil,' he said. 'It's a fossil of a fish.'

I stared at it for ages, but I couldn't see anything that looked anything like a fish – all I could see was a lot of dents and cracks.

'And here's a fern,' said Malcolm, pointing to the chunk of coal. Again, I couldn't see anything much, but I didn't tell Malcolm. I wondered if he needed new glasses. Malcolm went on holding things up.

'This is part of a clay pipe,' he said. 'This is some Victorian china and this is the top of an inkwell. Oh yes – and this is a bit of Roman mosaic.' He pointed to the scrunched-up metal things. 'But these are my prize possessions,' he said.

'What *are* they?' I asked.

'Roman coins,' said Malcolm. 'This one shows the Emperor Claudius – and this one here has the head of Julius Caesar. I got them for my birthday.'

I looked very hard, but they just looked like bits of old metal to me. I decided to change the subject.

'Would you like to see my football cards?' I asked. Malcolm sniffed.

'No thanks,' he said. 'Football's boring.'

He put on his pyjamas, then he took out a torch and a book about Roman villas and dived under the duvet.

I turned out the light and lay there in the darkness, thinking what a dead loss my cousin Malcolm was. Then I began to wonder what he was doing here. Why had my aunt and uncle dumped him on our doorstep? Perhaps he was such a dork they'd decided they'd had enough of him – him and his archaeological finds. Perhaps they'd gone on holiday.

But why had they been in such a hurry? And why hadn't they warned us they were coming? There was something very fishy going on. I began to doze off. Knock! Knock! An idea was trying to get into my head. Suddenly I was wide awake. I had it! My aunt and uncle were criminals – international criminals. The leaders of a gang. They'd committed the Crime of the Century and now they were making their getaway. They'd dumped Malcolm because they'd known he'd slow them down, always wanting to stop and dig things up. Perhaps they'd robbed a bank!

'Malcolm!' I hissed. 'Are you on the run?'

I could almost feel my cousin glaring at me in the dark.

'On the run?' he snorted. 'Don't be so silly!'

I decided to watch Malcolm like a hawk. Who knew? The police might be after him. Or perhaps Aunt Julia and Uncle Jimmy had double-crossed their accomplices, who even now were lurking around outside the house, waiting for their chance to grab Malcolm and hold him to ransom.

I must have dozed off, because the next thing I knew, Mum was drawing the curtains and calling:

'Rise and shine! Time to get ready for school!'

Chapter 4

'Class!' said Miss Wilson. 'We have a new member joining us today. I'd like you all to give a big welcome to Malcolm Weller, Josh's cousin.'

Thirty pairs of eyes swivelled and stared at Malcolm, who was sitting at the back of the room chewing a pencil and looking sulky. He didn't seem to appreciate his Big Welcome very much.

'We've been doing the Second World War, Malcolm,' said Miss Wilson, starting to pin our evacuee letters to the display board. 'If you look around you can see some of our work.'

The classroom looked wicked. We'd all been working on Second World War posters – some were about air raids, some about spies and others about

Digging for Victory. Kevin had done one of a rabbit holding a carrot. The rabbit had bionic eyes and above it, it said:

I was really proud of mine. It was all black and red and yellow – the sky was black, with bombs falling out of it, and underneath lots of houses were on fire. Right across the top I'd written:

'*Send your children from the city*
Or they'll be dead and that's a pity.'

I glanced at Malcolm. He didn't look impressed. Miss Wilson was pinning the last letters to the board.

'Oh, this is a good one, Josh!' she said, holding up my effort. 'I like the way it's all streaked – with tears, I suppose?'

Everyone laughed and I pretended to be doing up my shoelace. I was saved by a gentle tapping on the door.

'Ah! I know who this is!' said Miss Wilson, crossing to open it. She came back, followed by an old lady. 'Children!' she said. 'We've got a real treat this morning! This is Mrs Barker – say good morning.'

'Good morning, Mrs Barker,' we chanted, wondering why she was here.

'Mrs Barker actually attended this school during the war,' said Miss Wilson. 'She's kindly offered to tell you all about it. Over to you, Mrs Barker.'

Mrs Barker had silver hair and wore a purple cardigan. I'd seen her sometimes, going into the chip shop at the end of our road.

'I wasn't Mrs Barker then, of course,' she began in a creaky voice. 'I was Cissie Trubshaw.' Some of the class sniggered and Miss Wilson shot them a warning glance. 'I was nine when the war started.'

She began to tell us what it was like going to school in the war – about the air raids, the dogfights and the barrage balloons. How they were all issued with gas masks, which they never had to use. About their fathers going away to fight and what the sirens sounded like – how scary the Warning one was and how pleased they all were to hear  the All Clear. It was really interesting. When she'd finished, Miss Wilson said we could ask questions and a forest of hands shot up.

'Did you meet any spies?' asked Kevin.

'Not down our street,' said Mrs Barker. 'But there were lots of posters saying "Walls have Ears" – things like that.'

'And were you evacuated?' asked Joey Hilton.

'Some of my friends were,' said Mrs Barker. 'But quite a few of them came back. They missed their families. I didn't go, because my dad said we should all stay together.'

'Wasn't he fighting, then?' asked Lydia Gray.

'No,' said Mrs Barker. 'He was lucky. He had a bad chest, so they wouldn't have him in the army. He worked in a factory.'

At that moment, there was another tap on the door. It was the school secretary.

'Could Malcolm Weller come to the Head's office?' she asked. Malcolm sighed, heaved himself up and followed her out.

I put up my hand.

'What about air-raid shelters?' I asked. I'd watched a film at our local museum about schoolchildren filing down to an air-raid shelter. 'Was there an air-raid shelter at school?'

'Oh yes!' said Mrs Barker. 'Down at the bottom of the playground. It was in some old mine workings and it was quite deep. We did a lot of our lessons there. Some of us painted a mural on the walls. I think the teacher got us to do it to take our minds off things, and it certainly brightened up the place.'

'Cool!' said Eddie Lee. 'Where is it now, then?'

'I don't know,' said Mrs Barker. 'I think they filled it in at the end of the war.'

That was disappointing. Maxie Sykes put up his hand.

'It sounds really exciting!' he said. 'Was it fun in the war, Mrs Barker?'

'Fun?' said Mrs Barker thoughtfully. 'I don't know about "fun". I know some of the children liked watching dogfights and playing on the bomb sites and things like that. But I'll tell you this. I was really pleased when it was over. We had a party in our street – there were flags out all over the place.'

At that moment, Malcolm came back, still looking sulky and the bell went for break. We gave Mrs Barker a round of applause; some of us drummed on the tables and pounded our feet up and down. She looked pleased and gave us a big smile.

'Come along to the staff room, Mrs Barker,'

said Miss Wilson. 'I think we can find you a cup of tea and a biscuit – you deserve it.'

We all rushed out and stampeded around the playground. A group of kids stretched out their arms and pretended to be fighter planes, making a 'Wheeee!' sound. Some of us ran down to the bottom of the playground to where we thought the shelter might have been. Then we jumped around, listening for hollow, echoey sounds under the tarmac.

'This is definitely the place,' said Kevin and we lay down, with our ears to the ground, imagining all those kids from years ago, stuck down there, doing their lessons.

The ground was cold. I jumped up and strolled over to the high wire fence at the bottom of the playground. Behind it was a strip of land covered with trees called The Cut. You could get to it over my back fence and I often went there to play. Through the trees I could just make out the blue shed at the bottom of our yard and clothes flapping on the line.

'If this fence wasn't here,' I said to Kevin, giving it a shake. 'I could nip over The Cut and be at school in a minute or two – I could have an extra ten minutes in bed.'

'Oh well!' said Kevin. 'Brr! Brr! I'm a Spitfire! Come on, Josh! Let's go and have a dogfight!'

Chapter 5

'I don't believe it!' It was the weekend and Izzie was staring out of the kitchen window. 'What's that idiot up to now?'

I looked over her shoulder. It was Malcolm.

'Mum!' shouted Izzie. 'Come quick! Malcolm's digging a hole in the back yard!'

'Oh, it's all right. I said he could,' said Mum. 'Just as long as he fills it in again. He's doing his archaeology. I thought it would do him good to have an interest while he's here.'

'Archaeology!' snorted Izzie. 'Archaeology? What's he going to find in our yard?'

Things weren't going well between me and Malcolm. I'd tried to be friendly, but he just wasn't interested. It was much the same with everyone else – some of the kids in our class had tried to be nice to him, but he just gave them the cold shoulder. I'd been keeping an eye open for kidnappers on the way to school, but hadn't spotted any so far. I'd begun to think that if any *did* show up, they'd be welcome to him.

All the same, I sauntered down the yard. Malcolm was up to his knees in the hole. I peered in.

'Found anything yet?' I asked.

Malcolm looked up. He was wearing a stripy jumper. He wiped his glasses on his sleeve.

'Nothing of any significance,' he said.

I cast an eye over Malcolm's finds. There was a bone, one or two tin cans and a cup handle.

'I need to go down further,' said Malcolm, starting digging again. 'Please don't distract me.'

I wasn't bothered. I was going to the Saturday morning pictures with Kevin to see the new Simpsons film. I'd already asked Malcolm if he wanted to come, but he'd turned up his nose and

said he didn't see the point of the Simpsons. Too bad,
I thought – it's your loss, Malcolm.

When I got back, Malcolm was still digging. The
hole was much deeper now. All you could see of
Malcolm was his head and spadefuls of flying earth.
I went to have another look.

'Anything new?' I asked, peering down into the
hole.

Malcolm glared up at me, his face smeared with
dirt.

'No,' he said. 'Please go away. I'm concentrating.'

Mum came down the yard and joined me.

'I think it's time to stop,
now, Malcolm,' she said.
'This is getting a bit
dangerous. I don't want
the sides to cave in.
Come out now.'

Malcolm looked furious, but, all the same, he allowed Mum to haul him out.

'Josh will help you fill it in, won't you, Josh?' said Mum, walking off.

Huh! I took the spade and started shovelling. Malcolm just collected up his finds and disappeared.

Mum kept trying with Malcolm.

'Here's a programme you'll like, Malcolm!' she said that evening. 'What with your interest in history. It's called *Iron Age Village*. It's set on a remote Scottish island. We can all watch it together.'

I've never seen anyone look less keen on anything. Malcolm just grunted and turned away. And a bit later on, something strange happened. The remote control disappeared, just before *Iron Age Village* was about to start. We looked everywhere – behind the cushions, under the sofa and the chairs, in the kitchen. Everywhere. We even looked in the fridge, in case Mum had put it there during one of her absent-minded moments. But it seemed to have disappeared into thin air.

'Oh well,' said Mum. 'I'm sure it'll turn up. I don't know about you lot, but I'm going to curl up with a good book.'

And so we missed the first episode of *Iron Age Village*, but a bit later on that evening, I found the remote on the kitchen table – even though I was sure I'd looked there earlier.

'That's strange,' said Mum. 'Never mind – there's another episode on tomorrow at the same time. We can watch it then.'

But would you believe it? When we went to watch *Iron Age Village* the next evening, the remote was missing again. And then it turned up under the sofa when the programme was over. It was a complete mystery. Almost as big a mystery as Malcolm's missing parents.

Chapter 6

Later the next week, Miss Wilson announced she had a surprise for us.

'I want you to take these forms home and get your parents to sign them,' she said. 'Don't lose them – I know what you lot are like.'

'What are they for, miss?' asked Kevin.

'Everyone doing World War Two is going on a special train ride!' said Miss Wilson. 'It's an old steam train with old-fashioned carriages, just like the type the children would have been evacuated on during the war. There'll be other schools on it, too. We're going to meet it at the Junction.'

Everyone started whooping and jumping around, until Miss Wilson told us to quieten down.

'How long are we going away for, Miss Wilson?' asked Jason Potts. 'Is it for weeks?'

Miss Wilson laughed.

'No!' she said. 'It's just for a day. It's a day trip. It's to give you an idea of what it felt like to be evacuated. You can dress up if you like. Oh yes – and you all have to wear labels round your necks with your names on.'

Cool! I thought. I looked across at Malcolm. He didn't look excited – he just looked cross.

Mum looked at our forms that evening.

'Well, do you want to go?' she asked.

What a silly question!

'Of course I do!' I said. I looked at Malcolm, who was looking sulky.

'If you don't go, Malcolm,' I said. 'You'll probably have to stay behind in Mr Soames's class. He's really strict. He whirls kids round by the ears and throws them out of the window.'

'Oh, Josh!' said Mum. 'Don't listen to him, Malcolm. He got that out of *Matilda*. Do you want to go?'

'All right,' said Malcolm reluctantly. So Mum signed our forms.

'Now, Malcolm,' she said. 'I want a word with you. I know I said you could dig in the yard. But enough is enough. There are holes everywhere. I fell down one today when I went to put out the washing. I'm afraid you'll have to stop.'

Malcolm looked furious. He even stamped his foot.

'But I've had an idea,' said Mum. 'Josh, why don't you take him over to The Cut? He can dig away as much as he likes there.'

I thought this was a really bad idea. The Cut was my own special place. I met friends there and generally hung out. I didn't want to share it with Malcolm. Mum was looking at me.

'OK,' I said. 'I'll take you over at the weekend.'

And that's what I did. When Saturday came, I took Malcolm to the end of the yard; I noticed he was wearing his stripy jumper again. I got the spade from the shed and chucked it over the fence. Then I showed Malcolm how to climb up on the water butt.

After that, all you had to do was launch yourself over the fence and slide down the bank on the other side. Malcolm wasn't very good at this part. I had to shove him over, then he fell off the fence, rolled down the bank and landed up in the stream. It wasn't a very big stream – just a ditch, really.

But it was full of junk – supermarket trolleys, plastic bags and old hub caps – things like that. You could just step across if you felt like it, but I had a more exciting way of getting over. I grabbed a hanging branch and swung myself across. Malcolm fell off, of course, and landed in the stream again. I hauled him up the opposite bank.

'Well, this is The Cut,' I said, waving my arm. 'You can dig anywhere you like. It's a bit overgrown, though.'

It was true – I didn't think Malcolm would find many good places to dig. There was a level bit on the other side of the stream and then the ground rose sharply towards the fence at the top. You could just see the red brick walls of our school through the tangled branches.

Malcolm looked around. He didn't even say thank you.

'I shall dig here,' he said, pointing a dripping arm at a patch of open ground. 'You can go now. I don't want to be disturbed.'

He'd already started slicing away at the turf. I didn't mind since I was going to play football with Kevin. So I left him there in The Cut, digging away to his heart's content.

To tell the truth, I forgot all about Malcolm. I only remembered him later on, when I heard him calling me from the other side of the fence. I had to go down and haul him over. He was covered in mud and sand, but he looked really happy – the happiest I'd seen him so far.

He marched into the kitchen where Mum and Izzie were making a chocolate cake.

'Had a good day, Malcolm?' asked Mum. 'Yes, Izzie, you *can* scrape out the bowl.'

Malcolm drew himself to his full height. His glasses glittered.

'I've made a great discovery!' he announced.

We all stared at him.

'Yes!' said Malcolm. 'I've found a Roman villa!'

Chapter 7

'Have you, dear?' said Mum. 'That's nice.'

'A Roman villa?' said Izzie. 'In The Cut? I don't think so.'

'I have! I have!' said Malcolm, looking excited and angry at the same time.

'Calm down, Malcolm. I'm sure you have,' said Mum, shooting a warning glance at Izzie. 'I think you should go and get changed now. You can tell us all about it later.'

'That Malcolm's a weirdo,' said Izzie, when Malcolm had gone upstairs.

I didn't say anything. I secretly agreed with her, but I didn't want her to know that. I wondered what Malcolm's Roman villa was like. I imagined white pillars and wall paintings – could it be like that? I'd have a look at it tomorrow. It certainly seemed to have cheered him up, anyhow.

Malcolm's cheerfulness lasted till teatime.

'We'll have another go at watching *Iron Age Village*,' said Mum. 'It's on again tonight. It's one of those programmes where you vote to keep your favourite people in. It should be fun.'

I saw Malcolm's face fall. What was up with him? It was something to do with *Iron Age Village*, I was sure. So when I spotted him sidling out of the kitchen, I followed him. He went into the sitting room and I watched from the door as he picked up the remote and put it in his pocket. Whatever was he up to? I decided the time had come to act.

'What's your game then, Malcolm?' I asked, stepping into the room. Malcolm jumped and went red. He just stood there, looking guilty.

'It's a fair cop!' I said and I walked over and took the remote from his pocket. 'Why have you been hiding it?'

'Felt like it,' muttered Malcolm.

I couldn't get anything else out of him. I hung on to the remote until it was time for *Iron Age Village* and Mum herded us into the sitting room. I handed it over and Mum pressed the buttons.

Swirling mists drifted across the screen, mixed with the sound of bagpipes.

'Ah! "Songs of the Hebrides"!' said Mum, with a dreamy look on her face.

The mists rolled away and there was a rocky island, with a collection of huts in the middle.

'We bring you *Iron Age Village*!' said the announcer. 'The contest begins! The group have now been in the village for almost a fortnight. They've braved cold and storms. They've had to hunt for food and get used to cooking it over fires. But who's the ace survivor? Who isn't up to scratch? Who's in? Who's out? Tonight you, the viewers, get the chance to vote for your favourites.'

Malcolm got up to go, but Mum grabbed his arm and made him sit down again.

'Stay, Malcolm!' she said. 'This is *just* your sort of thing.'

The group was having a meeting in the biggest house. It was very smoky because there was an open fire in the middle of the room and it was difficult to see what was going on. There was quite a lot of bickering. Two men jumped up and shook their fists at each other, but the others pulled them apart.

After this, they went out and started work. Some were searching for food, some were weaving and others were herding sheep. It was blowing a gale and it looked as though it was freezing cold. Everyone was wrapped in tartan clothes and furs, so they all looked the same. A solitary figure sat on the seashore with a baited hook.

'Peter is waiting for a
catch,' whispered the
voiceover. 'The group
are relying on
him for their
meal tonight.'

Then the camera
swept away inland.
In the distance, a bearded
man was chasing some sheep.

'James is herding the flock,' said the
voiceover. 'He'll be shearing them later and giving
the fleece to the weavers.'

Suddenly a wild-looking woman thrust herself in
front of the camera. She started to sway from side to
side and I thought she
looked a bit mad.

'Jules is the self-
appointed bard
for the group,'
continued the
narration. 'She will
turn their exploits
into poetry and recite
it at meetings.'

'*Oh-oh-oh! Wild west wind!*' began the bard, waving her arms about. '*Oh blow! Thou bitter wind!*'

We all recognised her at the same moment. Mum sat bolt upright.

'Julia!' she cried. 'It's Julia!'

We all craned forward and stared at the screen – all except Malcolm, who tried to hide under a cushion.

'It is!' cried Izzie. 'It's Aunt Julia! It's your mum, Malcolm! What *does* she look like?'

A faint moan came from under the cushion. Behind Aunt Julia, we could see the bearded man going about his shepherding duties. He seemed to be wrestling with a sheep. His glasses had been knocked sideways and he looked desperate.

'It's Uncle Jimmy!' cried Izzy. 'Oh, please let me vote, Mum!'

She started to laugh – in fact, she laughed so much that she fell off the sofa.

Malcolm jumped up. His face was bright red.

'I'm going to bed!' he said in a muffled voice, and rushed out of the room.

Chapter 8

'Why didn't you *tell* us your mum and dad were going to be on that programme?' asked Izzie at breakfast the next morning.

Malcolm looked embarrassed and shoved half a slice of toast into his mouth.

'It was a secret,' he mumbled. 'It was in the contract. They were told not to let anyone know.'

'But why didn't you want to watch it?' asked Mum. 'It wasn't a secret once it had started, was it? And I thought you were really interested in history?'

Malcolm hesitated. He went bright red and looked very angry.

'That programme's a load of rubbish!' he burst

out. 'They've got it all wrong! I knew they would. It's not authentic!'

'What do you mean, "not authentic?" ' I asked.

'I mean it's not *accurate*,' said Malcolm, looking down his nose at me in a pitying sort of way. 'They wouldn't have lived like that in the Iron Age – in an isolated village. They'd be trading with other people. They wouldn't have spoken English. And my father was wearing *glasses* – they didn't have them then.'

'You don't know that,' I said. 'If they had iron, they could make the frames. And get some glass from somewhere.'

'Don't be silly, Josh!' said my cousin. 'Of course they couldn't. And do you think Iron Age people would have had a television crew following them around all the time?'

There was no answer to that.

'And there's something else,' muttered Malcolm. 'Something you don't know. Something awful . . .'

His voice tailed off. 'Can I get on with my excavation now, Auntie Pat? I'm really only interested in the Romans.'

And off he went. We had to wait until the next episode of *Iron Age Village* to find out what the Something Awful was. And I must say – it *was* awful. Downright horrendous, in fact.

I followed Malcolm down to The Cut. His excavation was going well. There weren't any signs of pillars or wall paintings, but he had uncovered a big flat expanse of what looked like a floor. I didn't say anything, but after a while Malcolm began to point things out to me.

'There's part of a wall,' he said. 'And here's a drainage channel. I daresay there's a hypercaust under this floor.'

'It looks like it's made of concrete,' I said. 'The Romans didn't have concrete, did they?'

'Well, that's where you're wrong,' said Malcolm, leaning on his spade. 'They did. They used it in quite a lot of their buildings.'

After a while, a few kids came drifting through the trees and started asking questions. I could see Malcolm wasn't too pleased about this. I went and got some rope from the shed. Then I wound it round trees and undergrowth until the whole area was cordoned off. I wrote a notice which said 'Keep Out. Important Arkylogical Site!' and hung it from the rope.

'You've spelled that wrong,' said Malcolm, but I wasn't really listening. I was too busy collecting entry money from people. Some of them snorted and walked off, but others turned out their pockets and gave me the odd coin or a toffee or two.

Malcolm began to enter into the spirit of things when I said we'd share the loot. He even stopped shovelling and gave the paying customers a short lecture about Roman villas.

★ ★ ★

'Let's see what your mum and dad are up to, Malcolm,' said Mum as she turned on the TV that evening.

There was the usual drifting mist and the sound of bagpipes. Then we learned that Peter the fisherman had got the least votes and was being sent off the island. He hadn't caught any fish and always looked grumpy. I suppose that's why people didn't like him. A helicopter arrived and airlifted him off to the mainland.

The villagers were having another meeting in the big hut. The flames flickered and the smoke billowed about the room. Someone started beating a drum and some of the group started shuffling around.

'Huh!' sniffed Izzie. 'Call that dancing?'

Then Aunt Julia recited a really boring poem about weaving cloth. There was a bit more dancing. And it was then that the Something Awful happened. Aunt Julia suddenly broke away from the group and rushed at the camera, so that her face was really close up, all smudged and sooty. She was holding a piece of paper.

'This is something I wrote earlier!' she said. 'It's for my little boy, Malcolm.' She waved at the camera. 'Hello, darling! Mummy's really missing you.'

I looked at Malcolm. He had turned bright red. Aunt Julia started to read from her scrap of paper.

'*I miss you so much, Malcolm darling!*

'*I think of you every night.*

'*I send you hundreds and hundreds of kisses*

'*And I hope that you're having a nice time*

'*And that everything's all right.*'

Izzie hooted with laughter and fell off the sofa again.

'What did I tell you?' muttered Malcolm. 'She said she was going to do it. Oh! I'm going to bed.'

He rushed off and left us sitting there. I began to feel sorry for Malcolm. What an awful thing to happen – your mum reading yucky poems about you on national television. We watched Uncle Jimmy wrestling with some more sheep and then two of the group began to fight.

Izzie was still laughing.

'Oh!' she gasped, clutching her sides. 'Oh! I'm going to get everyone in my class to vote to keep Uncle Jimmy and Aunt Julia in. What a laugh! I hope they stay on the island for ages.'

Mum turned off the TV and picked up her book.

'It wouldn't have been so bad,' she said, 'if it had been a decent poem. But that one didn't even scan.'

Chapter 9

The next morning, Mum had a quiet word with me and Izzie while Malcolm was cleaning his teeth.

'I don't want this thing about *Iron Age Village* to get around,' she said. 'It's embarrassing enough for Malcolm as it is. I've already promised him you won't say anything.'

Izzie began to pout.

'Can't I even tell Katya?' she asked. 'And Mia? And Lucy?'

'No!' said Mum. She sounded really stern. 'No one is to know. And if I find out either of you have been spreading it around, they'll be no pocket money. I mean it,' she added as Izzie opened her mouth to say something else.

We walked to school in silence. I could tell that Izzie was just bursting to tell people, but I knew she was saving up for a pony and she needed all the pocket money she could get. She only had enough for about half a hoof so far.

Malcolm went on with his digging. He was over the fence every afternoon after school. I noticed he'd rigged up a sort of climbing contraption on the other side, so he didn't need me to help him over.

'Roman villa?' said Izzie as we watched Malcolm disappearing over the fence with his spade. 'Honestly, Mum. He's *obsessed*.'

'I think it's taking his mind off his mum and dad,' said Mum. 'Leave him alone, Izzie.'

I followed Malcolm over the fence sometimes. I was quite interested. More and more of the villa had begun to appear.

'Do you really think it's Roman, Malcolm?' I asked.

Malcolm looked up, his face flushed.

'Don't be silly!' he said. 'Of course it is. Look! I've found the bath house.'

I looked, but all I could see was a slight dip in the floor.

Malcolm went on slicing at the turf. Suddenly he stopped, threw down the spade and dropped to his knees. He began scraping away with his hands.

'I knew it!' he cried. 'This proves it! Look! An inscription! Do you see? V ... I ... er ... C –'

'What does it mean?' I asked.

'I'm not sure,' said Malcolm. 'It's in Roman numerals, anyhow. VI is six. And C's a hundred. It probably means the year 106.'

Kids started to appear through the trees. Some came climbing over their fences, like us, but others wriggled in at the side of The Cut – there was an alleyway between the houses and a place where you could squeeze under the wire. News of

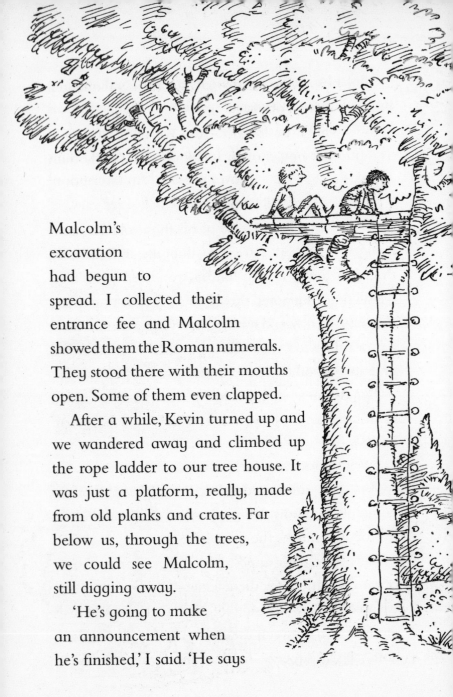

Malcolm's excavation had begun to spread. I collected their entrance fee and Malcolm showed them the Roman numerals. They stood there with their mouths open. Some of them even clapped.

After a while, Kevin turned up and we wandered away and climbed up the rope ladder to our tree house. It was just a platform, really, made from old planks and crates. Far below us, through the trees, we could see Malcolm, still digging away.

'He's going to make an announcement when he's finished,' I said. 'He says he's going to go to the museum and tell them all about it.'

'He'll be famous,' said Kevin. 'I wonder if you get any money for discovering a Roman villa?'

'Dunno,' I said. 'I suppose so.'

It was strange to think of all those old Romans living in The Cut. I tried to imagine it. Somehow, though, I found it very hard. I wondered what they did all day. I supposed they'd do a bit of fishing in the stream, which would have been a proper stream then, full of fish. Then when they got tired of that, they'd probably go off and have a battle with someone.

But the next day, Malcolm's excavations ended in disaster and we were left with a real battle on our hands.

Chapter 10

Iron Age Village seemed to be on every night of the week now. And things on the island were hotting up. First of all, everyone got food poisoning from a cauldron of rabbit stew and went around looking green and clutching their stomachs. When they recovered, rows broke out all over the place and two people escaped from the island in a small rowing boat. I kept waiting for Aunt Julia and Uncle Jimmy to be voted off, but they seemed to be really popular. Ginny the weaver was evicted and then Robert, the man who'd made the rabbit stew.

Malcolm didn't watch any more; he stayed in the kitchen and read his Roman villa book. So he almost missed Aunt Julia's latest poem. Almost.

He just happened to stick his head round the door as Aunt Julia ran up to the camera and screamed:

'I really miss you, Malcolm my darling!

'I can't get you out of my head.

'I keep wondering if anyone's giving you

'A goodnight kiss

'And tucking you up in bed.'

'Urgh!' choked Malcolm and rushed off.

Izzie hooted with laughter. I tried not to laugh, but it was very difficult.

'Really!' said Mum. 'I'm sure Julia could do better than that!'

Malcolm said nothing about his mum's new poem. It just seemed to make him more determined than ever to get on with his excavation.

A big crowd gathered in The Cut next day. I noticed that Dobber Dawson had turned up with some of his gang. They lurked around at the back of the crowd, shouting things out and laughing. I tried asking for their entrance fee, but Dobber said:

'Get lost, shrimp!'

Malcolm started giving one of his lectures, talking about the way the Romans built their villas.

'I shall probably uncover a mosaic soon,' he said.

'A mosaic, Four-Eyes?' said Dobber, pushing his way to the front of the crowd. His gang followed close behind.

'Yes, a Roman mosaic,' said Malcolm, glaring at him. 'And please don't interrupt me when I'm talking.'

He obviously knew nothing about Dobber Dawson, who went berserk. He ducked under the rope. Then he jumped down into the excavation and grabbed Malcolm by the front of his stripy jumper.

'Let go!' said Malcolm. But Dobber just held on and turned to the crowd.

'You lot are idiots!' he shouted. 'You really think this is a Roman villa? Well, it's not!'

'It is,' cried Malcolm. 'It is!'

'No, it's not!' growled Dobber and he gave Malcolm a shake. 'It's not a Roman villa. It's my grandad's pigsty.'

The crowd had gone silent. Some of them began to whisper.

'He kept his pigs here after the war!' said Dobber. 'He told me. And he never said anything about making a mosaic for them, Four-Eyes.'

Malcolm tried to pull away from Dobber, who held on tight.

'It is *definitely* of Roman origin!' he said. 'I have proof. Look! There's the date in Roman numerals. This villa was built in the year 106.'

Dobber looked where Malcolm was pointing, then he hooted with laughter.

'You nitwit!' he said. 'That's my grandad's name. He signed it in the cement. "V – I – C". Spells "Vic". Vic Dawson.' He turned to the crowd. 'You've been had!' he said.

Chapter 11

I'll say this for Malcolm, he just wouldn't give in. He glared at Dobber and said:

'You're an ignorant oik. You wouldn't know a Roman villa if it jumped up and bit you on the nose.'

What? I could hardly believe my ears. No one spoke to Dobber like that. And I mean No One.

'You've had it now, Four-Eyes!' snarled Dobber. I noticed the rest of his gang had sidled up behind him. 'We're gonna scalp you!'

Malcolm pulled away and managed to wriggle out of his jumper. Dobber was left holding it, looking furious.

'Come 'ere, you!' he roared.

I decided I had to do something. Even though my

cousin was such a dead loss, I couldn't let Dobber
and his friends scalp him, could I? I jumped down
next to Malcolm. I stared straight at Dobber and
stuck out my tongue.

'Pig face!' I said. It was all I could think of at the
time.

Dobber forgot Malcolm.

'You've had it now, Weller!' he yelled.

I just had time to hiss, 'Quick! Run for it!' in
Malcolm's ear and then I was off, tearing through
the trees, with Dobber and his gang after me.

I knew The Cut better than them, so I was able
to keep ahead. All the same, I soon realised someone
was gaining on me. I turned and there was Kevin,
pounding along behind me.

'The tree house!' he gasped.

I'd had the same idea. We reached it, shinned up the rope ladder and pulled it up after us.

We watched Dobber and his friends jumping around in rage below us. In the distance, I saw the flash of a white T-shirt as Malcolm scrambled away uphill. I'd thought he would make for the fence, but he must have had other ideas.

Dobber prowled around the tree. I heard him suggesting they burn it down, but it turned out they didn't have any matches. One of them said he was in the Scouts and could rub two sticks together. He tried it, but it didn't work.

Dobber shook his fist.

'Just you wait!' he yelled. Then he turned to his mates and said, 'Come on! Let's get the other one!'

They tore off through the trees and Kevin and I threw a few fir cones after them. After a while a crowd of kids gathered below us, muttering amongst themselves. Then one of them shouted:

'We want our money back!'

'And our sweets!' added another.

I'd already eaten most of the sweets, but I chucked down what I had in my pocket. There was a lot more muttering, then they drifted away.

Dobber and his friends couldn't find Malcolm.

Instead, they stuck his jumper on a pole and paraded round The Cut with it, shouting threats and insults. After a while it began to get dark and I heard Mum calling over the fence. Dobber and his friends lost interest. They threw down the jumper and ran off through the trees.

Malcolm appeared as if from nowhere. He came slithering and sliding down the slope, his hair full of twigs. He didn't say anything. He picked up his jumper and made for the fence.

'You're cousin's really weird, isn't he?' said Kevin. 'He didn't even say thanks.'

'He's like that,' I said.

As we were saying goodbye, Kevin said:

'See you on the train tomorrow, Josh.'

The school trip! I'd forgotten all about it.

Chapter 12

We all met up at the Junction the next morning. Miss Wilson had said we had to wear our safety jackets and the other schools did too, so the platform was a sea of yellow. We all carried old cases and satchels and rucksacks and Miss Wilson hung brown cardboard labels round our necks with our names on. Lots of grown-ups had come to see us off. Mum snuffled into a tissue and pretended to cry.

'Stop it, Mum!' I said.

Just at that moment there was a whistle and the train came steaming in. Kevin and I were standing next to the engine; it was shiny green with *The Flying Mallard* written on the side in gold letters. Inside, we could see the fire glowing as the stoker shovelled coal onto the flames. The driver leaned against the side of the cab and winked at us. Clouds of steam flew up and a strange, exciting smell filled the air.

What a life! I decided that when I was Prime Minister, I would abolish all electric railway lines and have only steam trains. Then I would resign and become a train driver. And Kevin could be my stoker.

Just then, Miss Wilson called us.

'On board, everyone!' she said.

We all crowded in. There were eight of us in our compartment, including Miss Wilson. I think Malcolm went in the one next door, but I didn't really notice. The engine gave a whistle and we were off.

I looked around the compartment. It wasn't like any railway carriage I'd been in before. There were mirrors on the walls and pictures of farms and trees. And above them – best of all! – two long luggage racks, made of net. We could hardly wait. The minute Miss Wilson wandered off down the corridor to see how the others were doing, we were up in those racks like a shot. It was wicked. I wondered if the old evacuees had done it. They'd all looked sad in the pictures I'd seen. I hoped they had – it would have cheered them up.

'Psst!' hissed Kevin, who was keeping a lookout and we all swung down as Miss Wilson came back along the corridor.

We sat and talked and watched the passing countryside and all the time great clouds of smoke whirled past the window, mixed with sparks.

'I want you to write about this when you get back,' said Miss Wilson. 'Try to imagine how the evacuees felt. They were leaving their homes and families and they didn't know where they were going. Or what was going to happen to them.'

I did try to imagine it, but it wasn't easy. They'd had no idea how long they'd be away and we were going to be home by four. The next thing we knew, the train ground to a halt and we'd reached our destination – the village of Oxley.

We formed a long yellow crocodile and marched down the road to the village hall. It was decorated with red, white and blue bunting and there were a lot of women gathered outside.

'Greetings, evacuees,' said one, stepping forward. 'We're the Womens' Institute of Oxley and we'd like to welcome you to our village. Please come inside for a real war-time dinner.'

The hall was packed with tables and chairs. A woman came out of the kitchen and said:

'I daresay you'd like to know what's on the menu. It's bacon pudding, potatoes and carrots. And after that, we have a nice carrot cake and custard.'

There was a chorus of 'Yuk!' all round, but when the bacon pudding arrived, everyone tucked in. It wasn't bad, either. And the carrot cake was yummy.

After we'd finished, one of the teachers announced we were going to have a quiz. The tables and chairs were cleared away and we formed a big circle round the hall. I spotted Malcolm, who was looking cross. Every so often, someone would grin and hiss, 'Pigsty!'

The quiz started. It was about shelters and barrage balloons and famous battles – things like that. After a while, I noticed that something strange was going on. Izzie's friend Lucy had a sister in our class, her name was Jodie. I'd seen her whispering to some of her friends earlier on; they'd been sniggering and looking at Malcolm. I'd thought it was about the pigsty. Then it began to get out of hand. Whispers went round and round the circle, until almost everyone was staring at Malcolm and giggling.

'Right!' said Miss Wilson, who didn't seem to have noticed. 'We're going to read some letters from evacuees now.'

Each of the teachers read out a letter and Miss Wilson finished up with a poem from a war-time picture book she said had belonged to her gran.

'*We're having such a lovely time*
'*Now we're evacuees.*
'*We run around the flowery fields*
'*And climb the orchard trees.*

'But remember,' added Miss Wilson. 'It wasn't all like that. Some of the evacuees had an awful time.'

Jodie put up her hand.

'Please, miss,' she said. 'I know a poem about an evacuee.'

All round the circle, kids were laughing and clapping their hands to their mouths.

'Well, let's hear it then, Jodie,' said Miss Wilson.

'It's from his mummy,' said Jodie in a silly voice and everyone laughed.

Then she began:

'*I miss you so much, Malcolm darling,*

'*I think of you every night . . .*'

It was Aunt Julia's poem! Izzie must have told Lucy about Malcolm and Lucy had told Jodie – and now everyone knew. Then, to my horror, at least half the room joined in.

'*I send you hundreds and hundreds of kisses,*' they bellowed.'*And I hope that you're having a nice time and that everything's all right!*'

Malcolm turned bright red. Then he put his head down and made a dash for the toilets.

Chapter 13

'I don't know what's going on here,' said Miss Wilson. It was ten minutes or so after Malcolm had rushed off. 'But you'd better go and get your cousin, Josh. The train leaves in half an hour.'

So I went into the toilets. One of them was locked and I could see Malcolm's feet under the door.

'Are you coming out, Malcolm?' I called. 'We've got to leave soon.'

'Clear off!' shouted Malcolm. 'Go away. I don't want to talk to you.'

'Come on, Malcolm,' I said and I kneeled down and peered up at him. He was still red in the face.

'I'm never talking to you again!' he shouted.

'You told them. You told them all about my mum and dad. You taught them that poem!'

'I didn't!' I said indignantly. 'It wasn't me. It must have been Izzie.'

'I don't believe you!' growled Malcolm. 'Go away!'

I had to go back and tell Miss Wilson that Malcolm wouldn't come out. In the end, she had to send Mr Poole in to get him. Malcolm came out looking crosser than ever.

I was cross, too – cross with Izzie. She'd no idea how much trouble she'd caused.

'Is that really your aunt and uncle on *Iron Age Village*?' asked Kevin on the way home.

I grunted. I didn't feel like talking – to tell the truth, I felt a bit sick.

It wasn't long before we were pulling into the Junction. There was a crowd of parents waiting on the platform and they started waving to us as we tumbled off the train.

'Wait a moment, class!' said Miss Wilson. 'I have to do a head count. Then you can go home.'

Miss Wilson counted us and looked puzzled. She did it again and whispered to Mr Poole, who counted us, too. Miss Wilson took out the register and went through it. She called my name and I answered. Then she called, 'Malcolm Weller!' There was no reply.

Mr Poole ran down the platform and shouted at the engine driver, who was starting to get up steam.

'Stop the train!' he yelled. 'One of the children is missing!'

Our class was herded into the waiting room while Miss Wilson and Mr Poole walked up and down the train. Miss Wilson came out, carrying a yellow jacket.

'I found it in one of the toilets,' she said.

The parents were milling around outside the waiting room. Mum pushed forward, looking pale, with Izzie dragging along behind her.

'It's Malcolm, isn't it?' she said. 'What's happened?'

'We don't know,' said Miss Wilson. 'He's just disappeared.'

The police arrived and asked questions – when had we last seen Malcolm and how did he seem? It was strange – no one could remember having seen him after the train started. Miss Wilson said he'd been very upset in Oxley, so they started questioning us about that and gradually the whole story came out.

Izzie shifted about and looked guilty and Mum gave her a funny look.

'That poor child!' she said. 'He must have felt awful.'

'Do you think he might have fallen out of the train, Mrs Weller?' asked Colin Briggs.

'Do be quiet, Colin!' said Miss Wilson, glaring at him. 'All the doors were locked.'

The police asked Mum if she had any idea where he might have gone. They'd already sent someone round to our house, and he wasn't there.

'Well, I suppose he could have gone to Scotland to see his mum and dad,' said Mum doubtfully. 'Or he might have gone back to his own home. He had some money on him. He could have caught a train – or a bus. Oh! What are we going to do?'

'The best thing you *can* do, Mrs Weller,' said a policeman, patting her on the shoulder, 'is go home and wait – in case he turns up. You never know.'

So we went home. I kept hoping that Malcolm would be sitting on the doorstep, waiting for us, but he wasn't. And when I went upstairs, I had a shock. All Malcolm's things were gone, including his archaeological finds.

'He must have planned this,' said Mum. 'Packed everything this morning.'

'Then it wasn't the poem that upset him after all,' said Izzie, who'd had a good telling-off from Mum. 'It was probably all that stuff with the pigsty. So it's your fault, Josh.'

'How's it my fault?' I started. 'I only –'

'Oh, stop it, you two!' cried Mum. 'Just stop it. I'll have to let Jimmy and Julia know. However am I going to tell them?'

Chapter 14

Mum managed to contact the television company, though it took her a while. I listened to her talking to them on the phone. 'Oh no!' she said every so often. 'How awful!'

She came back with a long face. It seemed the north of Scotland was being lashed by towering waves and hurricane-force winds. So there was no hope of getting anyone off the island – it was much too dangerous for boats and even the helicopter couldn't get through.

'They said there'd be no point in worrying them,' she said. 'Oh dear! This is terrible!'

That evening we watched a special edition of *Iron Age Village*. Storms battered the island and things looked really grim. The villagers didn't venture out. Every so often you'd see a head poking round a door and then they'd disappear again. The roof blew off one of the huts and they all ended up sheltering in the big Meeting Hut.

Aunt Julia read a poem about storms, and after that, a shorter one, all about Malcolm and what lovely golden curls he had when he was a baby. I was glad Malcolm had missed that one.

'Oh, poor Julia!' said Mum. 'If only she knew!'

The police phoned and told Mum they were coming round the next day to ask us a few questions. They said they wanted a word with me, so Mum kept me home from school. I was dead worried, I can tell you.

They arrived in the afternoon. There was no news of Malcolm. He hadn't been spotted on any trains or buses. They'd checked the family home and he hadn't gone there. I heard them whispering to Mum that they'd even searched the train tracks, but found nothing. It was as though Malcolm had disappeared into thin air.

They went through the whole story again with me. I had to tell them about *Iron Age Village*, about the pigsty and what had happened in the village hall at Oxley. About how everyone had shouted out Aunt Julia's poem and how Malcolm had turned red and locked himself in the toilets.

'Are you *sure* you didn't say anything, Josh?' asked Mum.

'Of course I didn't,' I said. 'I wasn't too keen on people knowing about Aunt Julia, either.'

'Hmm. I could *murder* Izzie,' said Mum.

'I'd rather you didn't, madam,' said one of the policemen.

They finished their questions and then they said they'd like to look at Malcolm's excavation.

'Josh will show you, won't you, Josh?' said Mum.

So I took them over the fence. They weren't very fit and they both rolled into the stream. They had a quick look at the pigsty and wandered around The Cut for a while.

I could see they weren't too keen on staying long; they were both soaking wet.

I watched them climb back over the fence.

'Are you coming, sonny?' asked one.

'Nah,' I said. 'I'll just stay here for a while.'

I decided to have a think. I went and sat down on the edge of the excavation. Whatever could have happened to Malcolm? It suddenly struck me that he must have felt a bit like an evacuee himself, cut off from his parents like that. Of course, he wouldn't have had to worry about them being bombed but he would have been worried all the time about his mum reading out her awful poems. He must have felt terrible, mustn't he?

As I sat there, thinking about all this, something caught my eye. It was lying on the ground, next to Grandad Dawson's signature. I knelt down to have a closer look.

My heart skipped a beat and I stretched out my hand and picked it up. It was a coin – a bent Roman coin. And on it I could just make out the head of Julius Caesar.

Chapter 15

I could hardly believe my eyes. How had that got there? That coin had been on Malcolm's table yesterday morning, and now everything had gone, along with Malcolm. What did it all mean?

It took me a while to work it out. Malcolm had been here. And he must have been here after he got off the train. I got up and looked around. I suppose I'd half hoped to see Malcolm coming towards me through the trees. I decided to climb up to the tree house, in case he was there, but of course he wasn't.

As I sat there, I thought about Dobber dancing round the tree with his mates, and almost in the same moment I remembered the flash of Malcolm's white T-shirt as he scrambled up the bank. He'd found somewhere to hide, hadn't he? I wondered where. I decided to investigate.

I slid down the ladder and started to climb the bank where I'd last seen my cousin. It was quite steep – brambles caught at my clothes and tugged me back and I was out of breath by the time I reached the top. I started to search around amongst the tangle of weeds and bushes.

I'd almost decided to give up and go home for tea when I saw the second coin. I bent to pick it up, and at the same moment I saw the tunnel. It was half hidden by long grass and disappeared into the heart of a holly bush. I took a deep breath and began to push my way through.

It wasn't easy; the bush was prickly and it was getting darker all the time. I started to get scared. I stopped – and a good thing, too, because right in front of me was a gaping hole. Another second and

I'd have been down it. I was about to start backing out when something caught my eye. Hanging on a twig above the hole was a pair of glasses. Malcolm's glasses! I recognised the sticky tape round one of the handles. I edged forward again and leaned over the black space.

'Malcolm!' I called.

No answer.

I leaned out further and shouted again. But this time I leaned too far. The ground gave way beneath me and the next thing I knew I was falling downwards into pitch darkness.

I landed with a thud on a pile of sand and rolled on downwards. When I finally came to a stop, I just lay there, trying to gather my wits. I sat up slowly and, to my surprise, I saw a light. It was playing across the walls of what seemed to be a sandy tunnel. And it was coming nearer and nearer.

'Hello!' said a quavery voice. 'Who is it?'

It was Malcolm!

'It's me – Josh – you idiot!' I said. 'What are you doing down here?'

'The same as you, I suppose,' said my cousin as he shone the torch at me. 'I fell in. Are you hurt?'

I stood up and rubbed my back. I was all in one piece.

'I'm OK,' I said. 'What about you?'

'Er – have you got anything to eat?' asked Malcolm. 'I haven't had anything since the bacon pudding.'

I felt in my pocket and found two toffees. I gave them to Malcolm and he gobbled them up.

'We've got to get out of here,' I said.

'We can't,' said Malcolm. 'We're trapped.'

He shone his torch upwards and I saw what he meant. Even if you climbed up the pile of sand, it was still a long way to the top and there was an overhang which would make climbing out almost impossible.

'You'd better come to my camp,' said Malcolm. 'We can talk there.'

I followed him down the sandstone tunnel and he stopped by a small cave that had been scooped into the wall. I noticed that he'd padded it out with the contents of his rucksack – his anorak, T-shirts and spare trousers. He was wearing his stripy jumper.

'Is this where you stayed last night?' I asked.

'Yes,' said Malcolm. 'And I think we'd better stay here tonight, too.'

So we snuggled down in the cave and Malcolm began to tell me how he'd managed his great disappearing act.

Chapter 16

'I didn't mean to come here,' said Malcolm. 'It was an accident.'

'What do you mean "an accident"?' I asked.

Then Malcolm explained what had happened. He'd packed everything into his rucksack before we'd left for the Junction. He said he'd had a plan.

'I couldn't bear it any longer,' he said. 'There were Mum's poems – and the pigsty and –'

He hesitated.

'Yes?' I prompted.

'It was your sister Izzie,' said Malcolm. 'I can't stand her.'

'That's OK,' I said. 'I'm not too keen on her myself.'

Malcolm said that halfway through the train journey, he'd gone along the corridor and locked himself in the toilet. No one came looking for him and when we pulled into the Junction, he came out, leaving his jacket behind. Then he made his way through the crowds, found the side exit and just slipped away. No one seemed to notice him. Then he ran for all he was worth.

'I was going to catch the bus at the end of your road,' he said. 'And I was going to go back home – I've got a key. I thought I'd hide there till Mum and Dad came off that awful island.'

'So how come you ended up in The Cut?' I asked.

'Well, I was on my way to the bus stop,' said Malcolm, 'When I saw that Dobber Dawson outside the chippie on the corner of your road. He had a load of mates with him and I was sure they'd seen me. I was right next to that alleyway, so I ran down it into The Cut.'

Aha! That explained a lot.

'And I remembered the place I'd hidden the other day,' said Malcolm. 'So I headed for it again. And you know what happened next.'

We sat there in the darkness. I was sure I could hear bats moving about. Malcolm had switched off his torch, because he wanted to save the batteries.

'How did you find me?' he asked.

I didn't say anything. Instead, I felt in my pocket and took out the Roman coins. Then I pressed them into his hand.

'Oh!' said Malcolm. 'They must have fallen out of my rucksack.'

I waited for him to say thanks but of course, being Malcolm, I don't think it occurred to him.

'We've got to find a way out of here tomorrow,' I said.

Malcolm didn't reply. I could feel him quivering

next to me in the darkness and at first I thought he was crying. What a wimp!

'Cheer up, Malcolm!' I said, giving him a nudge. 'I'll think of something. Don't worry.'

'I'm not worried,' said Malcolm in a strange voice, and I realised that he wasn't crying at all – he was shivering with excitement. 'I want to stay down here, Josh.'

What? Had he gone mad? Perhaps the darkness and the bats had tipped him over the edge.

'What do you mean, you want to stay?' I asked.

'I can't leave until I've finished my investigations!' said Malcolm. 'You can help me, Josh.' His voice rose to a triumphant squeak. 'I'll show you tomorrow. I've made the greatest discovery of my life!'

Chapter 17

I fell asleep quite quickly. I dreamed giant bats were flying around me, perching on my head and squeaking, 'The greatest discovery of my life!'

I woke up once or twice and I'm sure I heard Malcolm muttering the same thing: 'The greatest discovery of my life!'

I woke again. There was no way of knowing if it was day or night down there, but this time, it felt like morning.

'Time to get going, Malcolm,' I said, but my cousin had already got going. When I went to nudge him, my elbow met empty air. Where had he gone this time? It was a horrible feeling, sitting there in the dark, listening to the bats rustling above me.

After a while, I spotted a torch flashing on and off in the distance. I got up and made my way towards it.

'Malcolm!' I called as I stumbled along.

'Here!' came the reply, echoing down the tunnel. 'Come and see what I've found.'

I stepped through a doorway with carved pillars on either side. The tunnel opened out into a giant cavern. Malcolm came towards me, flashing his torch. I noticed that he was still trembling with excitement.

'Would you believe it?' he crowed. 'I'm going to be famous! Have you heard of Pompeii, Josh? The terracotta army? Tutankhamun's tomb?' He didn't wait for me to answer, but rushed on, 'This beats all of those! This is the best moment of my life!'

'But what *is* it?' I asked, shivering, because it was cold in the cave.

'It's a Roman crypt!' whispered Malcolm, catching at my coat. 'There's probably a ruined villa above us – just look at this!'

He swept his torch round the walls and I saw that they were covered with fantastic paintings. The colours – reds, blues, yellows and greens – were still very bright.

'It's a Roman mural!' said Malcolm. 'There's gardens and roman soldiers and eagles. No one's ever seen anything like it!'

I wished we could see the Roman mural all at once, but we could only examine it one bit at a time. Malcolm went on sweeping his torch around the walls and talking about the newspapers and the British Museum and how he was going to be famous. Suddenly I noticed something that didn't seem quite right.

'Look!' I said. 'Isn't that someone riding a bicycle?'

Malcolm peered at the wall.

'Yes!' he cried. 'Yes, it is!' He started to gambol about the cave. 'Yes!' he yelled again, punching the air. 'So the Romans had bicycles! I always knew it – they were fantastic inventors!'

'Give me the torch,' I said and grabbed it from him. I shone the beam about the walls. I could see children on scooters and people with umbrellas. There was even a car or two.

'Malcolm,' I said. 'I don't think this is Roman.'

'What do you mean?' said Malcolm, with a sneer in his voice. 'Of *course* it's Roman! What else could it be?'

'Well, look at this,' I said and beamed the torch upwards. 'What do you think this is, up in the sky?'

'It's a bird of prey,' said Malcolm. 'Probably an eagle. The legions carried them into battle. It's a *symbol*, Josh. Do you know what that means?'

'Malcolm! Look!' I said. 'Look closer! It's an aeroplane.'

Malcolm screwed up his eyes and I remembered that he hadn't got his glasses. I'd left them hanging on the twig.

I'd thought the aeroplane would settle it once and for all; but instead, Malcolm started capering about again and yelling at the top of his voice.

'So they had *aeroplanes* too!' he cried. 'This is going to cause a sensation!'

'How do you think they flew them?' I asked. 'With wind-up rubber bands?'

'Don't be silly,' said Malcolm. 'They didn't have rubber then, you idiot. No doubt they used some other method of propulsion.'

'Malcolm,' I said, grabbing his arm. 'You haven't got your glasses, have you? Just look at this.'

And I guided him to some writing at the base of the wall.

'Aha! An inscription!' said Malcolm. 'It's a pity you don't understand Latin, Josh.'

'I don't need to,' I said and I began to read aloud, slowly and very carefully. 'Mr . . . Pellow's . . . class . . . May . . . 1942.'

Chapter 18

There was a long silence. At last, Malcolm spoke.

'I don't understand,' he said.

'Look around you,' I said, grasping his arm. 'Don't you know what this is?'

'What?' said Malcolm, sounding sulky.

'It's an air-raid shelter!' I said. 'Don't you remember Mrs Barker telling us about it in class?'

'No,' said Malcolm.

Then I remembered – Malcolm had missed the bit about the shelter; the school secretary had hauled him off to the Head halfway through Mrs Barker's talk.

'The kids painted this while they were down here in the war,' I said.

Malcolm was silent and I had a feeling he wasn't convinced. I stepped forward, meaning to show him the painting of the car and trod on something creaky. Ugh! What was it? A dead bat? I shone the torch downwards at The Thing. It was flat, made of decaying rubber and had a sort of filter attached to it. I'd seen one in the museum. I picked it up and waved it at Malcolm.

'It's a gas mask!' I said.

Malcolm just made a sort of huffing sound. And it was at that point that the torch batteries ran out.

We stood there, plunged into darkness.

'We've got to get out!' I said. 'Hold onto my top, Malcolm.'

We groped our way out of the cavern and along the tunnel. We passed our camp and stumbled on in the dark until we reached the sandy slope where we'd fallen in. And then I saw the best sight I'd seen for a long time – a patch of light, high above us. It was weak and wavery, but daylight just the same.

'It's morning!' I said. 'They'll be looking for us. We've got to get up there.'

'But how?' said Malcolm. 'I've tried. It's too high.'

I thought for a while.

'There's two of us now,' I said. 'What about if you stand on my shoulders?'

'I can't,' said Malcolm. 'I suffer from vertigo.'

There was just enough light coming from above to reveal the pile of sand at the bottom of the shaft.

'We could make a sort of platform on top of this,' I said. 'And use it to stand on.'

So for the next hour or so, we scrabbled away with our hands, firming and building up the sand. Malcolm grumbled all the time, but at last we had a level area.

'Now!' I said and I climbed up and pulled Malcolm after me. I tried my best to hoist him up towards the top, but he kept swaying about and yelling, 'No! No! Put me down!' So I gave up and lowered him back to the ledge.

'It's no use,' I said. 'I'll have to stand on you.'

'No way!' said Malcolm. 'You're too heavy. I'm not strong enough.'

But I climbed up on him anyway, while he grumbled and moaned beneath me and wobbled about, going 'Ow!' and 'Ouch!' There were a lot of tree roots hanging down and I grabbed them and pulled myself up. Soon I was standing upright on Malcolm's shoulders. How was I going to get round the overhang? I felt round it and grabbed a root.

'Aargh!' shrieked Malcolm and fell over. I was left there, dangling in mid-air. But just above me was daylight. And fresh air. I knew I wasn't going to be able to climb out – I'd never do it. But I made one last effort. I hauled myself up with my arms so that my face was almost level with the top of the hole. Then I tilted back my head.

'Help! Help!' I shouted. 'We're here!'

Then my arms gave way and I slithered back to the floor.

We lay there in a heap.

'We've had it,' said Malcolm. 'Centuries from now, archaeologists will discover this place and find our bones.'

'Shut up, Malcolm!' I said.

We sat there in complete silence, with the faint green light filtering through above us. I secretly thought Malcolm might be right. I've never felt so hopeless in my life.

Then a wonderful thing happened. Suddenly the light was blotted out and a voice rang out above us. 'Hello! Hello? Is there anybody there?'

Chapter 19

They brought a ladder and helped us out. They told us one of the search party had been standing next to the bush when I shouted and he'd almost jumped out of his skin.

I'll never forget that feeling when we climbed out into the open air. The first thing I noticed was that they'd chopped down the holly bush. And the next thing was that The Cut was crawling with people. Someone gave Malcolm back his glasses and Mum came rushing forwards and flung her arms round us. It was really embarrassing.

'You're safe!' she cried. 'What do you *mean* by disappearing like that? Oh! I'm so glad you're back! Oh! I could strangle you!'

Make your mind up, Mum.

There was even a reporter from the local paper there. He pushed his way through the crowd.

'Josh! Malcolm!' he shouted. 'Can I have an exclusive?'

'Keep back, sir,' said a policeman. 'Don't you think these boys have been through enough already?'

It was then that Malcolm really surprised me. He shoved me to one side and stepped forward.

'No!' he said. 'It's all right! Let me speak to him.'

The crowd fell silent. *What was he going to say?* I wondered. *Perhaps something along the lines of 'I'd really like to thank my cousin Josh for getting us out of this hole. If it hadn't been for him, we wouldn't be standing here now'.*

But did he heck. What he actually said was this:

'I have an important announcement to make. I'm an archaeologist. I'm specially interested in World War II.'

What? That was the first I'd heard of it. I'd thought it was the Romans Malcolm was keen on. He was still speaking.

'I've made a discovery,' he went on. 'I've found a Second World War air-raid shelter. I've been searching for it for ages.' He pointed at the hole. 'It's down there and there's the most amazing murals and a gas mask.'

The reporter was scribbling away for all he was worth.

'Yes!' continued my cousin. 'The school used it in the war. The children painted the mural.'

The little rat! I stood there, lost for words.

But you thought it was Roman, I wanted to say. *It was me who told you it was an air-raid shelter!*

I opened my mouth to speak, but then I thought better of it and closed it again. I remembered what an awful time Malcolm had been having, what with Aunt Julia's poems and everything else and I just felt sorry for him.

Oh, let him get on with it, I thought and turned away.

My mum stepped forward.

'Never mind about the old air-raid shelter,' she said. 'Come on, you two – I'm taking you home.'

It was nice being back in the warm. Mum cooked us the best breakfast I've ever had – bacon, sausages, tomatoes and fried bread. It was wicked.

'You need to keep your strength up,' she said.

The police came round and asked us a few questions and then later on the reporter turned up with a photographer.

'Oh no – I don't think so,' said Mum.

'Please, Auntie Pat – *please!*' begged Malcolm and in the end Mum gave in and let them take photos of us.

Izzie came in while this was going on.

'Oh, so they're back, then,' she said. 'That's a pity.'

'And who are you?' asked the reporter.

'Izzie Weller,' said my sister, giving a twirl. 'I'm going to be a model. Would you like to take my picture?'

'Not today, thanks,' said the photographer and he packed up his kit and went off with the reporter.

The *Examiner* was full of it the next day. 'Boy Archaeologist's Amazing Find!' said the headline. 'Old School Air-raid Shelter Rediscovered.'

Malcolm's photo was plastered across the front page. He had a big smirk on his face. I flicked through the paper, but there was hardly any mention of me at all. 'Local History Society in Ecstasies' said another heading. There was even a picture of Mrs Barker. Underneath it said: 'A child in the War – a former pupil speaks.'

Mum kept us home for the rest of the week, which was cool, except I had to listen to Malcolm wittering on about 'his' air-raid shelter and watch him arranging his press cuttings in a scrap book. So I was quite relieved when Monday arrived.

'Welcome back, Malcolm! And you, too, Josh!' said Miss Wilson. I waited for her to tell Malcolm off for running away, but instead she just beamed at him and said, 'A great discovery, Malcolm! We've got a surprise for you.'

A bald-headed man, who'd been sitting next to her, got up.

'I'm from the Local History Society!' he said. 'Malcolm Weller – please step forward!'

He pinned a badge on Malcolm's chest, saying 'Young Archaeologist of the Year' and everyone clapped.

The History Man told us that their society had been down in the caves, exploring and taking photos and they were going to make a book of them. And Miss Wilson chipped in and said that the PTA were going to club together and open up the old air-raid shelter entrance from the school playground.

'Then we can use it for Second World War lessons!' she said. 'It's so exciting! I can hardly wait!'

Something even more exciting was waiting for Malcolm when we got home. Aunt Julia and Uncle Jimmy were there! Uncle Jimmy's beard had disappeared and they both looked as though they'd had a good wash. They told us that all the roofs on the village houses had blown away and that everyone had caught cold. They'd all shouted: 'We're Iron Age Villagers – Get us out of here!' So the television company had evacuated them once the storms had died down. My aunt and uncle were real evacuees!

'Did you like my poems, darling?' asked Aunt Julia.

'Huh!' said Malcolm and started showing them his press cuttings.

Chapter 20

I didn't tell anyone except Kevin what had really happened in the cave, and I swore him to secrecy. So here we were, at half term, up in the tree house. The sun was shining and the leaves were falling all around us and it was great to be off school. At the top of the slope, half hidden by the trees, a big yellow digger was working away in the playground. It was opening up the old entrance to the air-raid shelter. They'd filled in the hole I'd fallen down.

Far below us, some Year Twos were playing marbles on the floor of the pigsty. Kevin and I had our Hallowe'en masks with us – I was a Cyberman and Kevin was a ghoul. We'd thought we might try them out on the little kids later. We were going to come wailing through the trees and give them a fright. But then one or two of their big sisters turned up so we changed our minds.

Suddenly, the peace was shattered by a lot of screaming. It was coming from our back yard. It went a bit like this:

'Yaaah! It's not fair! Yaaaaaah!'

'What's up with your sister?' asked Kevin.

'Oh,' I said. 'Mum's just found out she's made hundreds of phone calls. She was trying to keep Malcolm's mum and dad on the island. There's an enormous bill. Mum says she can't have any more pocket money till the summer and she's got to hand over all her savings.'

'So no chance of that pony, then?' said Kevin, who was fond of animals.

'Nope!' I said. 'None at all.'

'What about a hamster?' asked Kevin.

'She couldn't even afford one of its whiskers,' I said.

We sat there, swapping masks, and all the time the digger rumbled away in the background.

'When they've finished,' said Kevin, 'there's going to be a grand opening ceremony, with the Mayor and the History Society and Mrs Barker and everyone. We might even get a day off.'

'They're asking Malcolm back,' I said. 'He's going to cut the ribbon.'

'I bet you'll be pleased to see him again. *Not*,' said Kevin.

'Oh, he wasn't that bad,' I said.

Kevin snorted. I knew he thought I should have gone to the papers and exposed Malcolm's lying. I wasn't bothered. I felt in my pocket.

'Besides,' I said. 'He gave me a leaving present.'

I held out my hand and Kevin stared.

'Yeah! Great!' he said at last. 'A bit of bent tin? I don't call that much of a present.'

'That's where you're wrong, Kevin!' I said. 'It's not a bit of tin. It's a Roman coin. Look! Here's the head of Julius Caesar!'